The COMING of GRAY OWL

by IDA MAY HOBBS

Illustrated by David W. Wilson

Edited by Lillian B. Lang, Ph.D.
Fort Lewis College, Durango, Colorado.

Design: Graphic Interpretations

MESA VERDE MUSEUM ASSOCIATION, INC.
MESA VERDE NATIONAL PARK, COLORADO

· Acknowledgements ·

The first acknowledgement belongs to my daughters Laura, Elizabeth, Peggy, and Becky because they were understanding and patient when I was too preoccupied to cook their dinner or tend to their needs. Second, my parents, Carnie and Madge Williams, have always believed in me and given me their loving support. Several others also gave me their support as well as helpful suggestions for this book. Jerry Hobbs, who was a seasonal park ranger at Mesa Verde National Park, willingly gave me his support. The final acknowledgement is to the Institute of Children's Literature and to my instructor, Terri Martini, for their invaluable help in the writing of this book.

· Contents ·

To my
daughters,
Laura, Elizabeth,
Peggy and Becky

Copyright ©1987 by Mesa Verde Museum Association, Inc.

Library of Congress Number: 86-063484
ISBN 0-937062-09-X

First Edition 1987
Second Printing 1990

Printed in the United States of America.

This book is printed on
acid-free, archival paper
made from 50 percent
recycled stock.

• Chapter I •
The Trader

The little boy could not take his eyes off the brown, wrinkled face of the trader sitting across the fire-pit from him. He leaned forward, eager to hear every word the old man was saying about the distant lands and waters.

"Far from here, toward the setting sun, is water so big you can not see across it," he said, looking at the boy and the other children gathered around the fire. He drew an object from his pouch. "This shell came from the edge of that water," he explained, as he held it up for them to see. The rich pearl color on the inside of the shell glowed softly in the firelight. "In trade, it will bring a good price," he smiled as he nodded at the shell.

The little boy pulled his woven turkey-feather blanket closer around his bare shoulders, pleased with its warmth. His straight black hair, chopped off just below his ears, fell forward to frame his round face. He did not think he looked like his name, with such a round face. It should be long and lean, like that of the fox for whom he was named. "I should not be called 'Little Fox,'" he thought. "My round face makes me look like an owl, so I should be called 'Little Owl.'" Then he turned his dark brown eyes, slanted slightly toward the hair line, back to the trader once again. They were filled with wonder as he listened to the trader describe his travels.

"I have seen vast stretches of land, where only grass grows, and tall mountains covered with snow." He poked at the fire, needed to keep away the chill of early morning air in the cave where the warm spring sunshine would not reach until early afternoon. Little Fox spoke up.

"Tell us more about the things you have seen where you have traveled." He waited for the old man to speak again.

"I have seen many animals, some in large herds that would cover the whole mesa above this cave. I saw rivers so wide I could not cross them," the trader replied.

"Do people live there and hunt such animals?" asked Running Deer, Little Fox's cousin, who was sitting next to him.

"Yes," the trader nodded. "To the south live people like you, but they do not live in caves in the cliffs." He went on to explain. "They live in the flat river bottoms. Your people trade with them. I have also seen people who are not like you. They do not plant crops. They carry their homes with them and they live mostly in the

mountains. These people roam the land north of here looking for food and hunting animals."

"What do they look like?" asked Little Fox.

The trader thought for a while. "They are taller than your people," he began. "They do not have the backs of their heads flattened as you do." He paused.

Little Fox's younger sister, Butterfly Girl, laughed. "How funny they must look!" The other girls in the group giggled.

Little Fox frowned. "How silly girls are," he thought. Turning his attention back to the trader, he asked what he was sure was a grown-up question. "Do you trade with these people?"

Once again the trader nodded. "Yes, but I met a tribe a few days back, that is not always friendly. They have many fights with each other, and sometimes they attack the villages of your people." He sat gazing into the fire for a few minutes, then he picked up his bulging pack and rose to leave.

The children walked along with him, pleading for him to stay, to tell them more of the wonders he had seen. He said he had other places to go and other people to see and could stay no longer. The children stopped at the edge of the courtyard and watched as the old trader carefully climbed down the sheer cliff face to the canyon floor below. He was not agile and swift like their fathers and older brothers. He looked carefully where he positioned each foot and the knuckles of his hands were white as he held tightly to the tiny finger holds. From the canyon's floor, he looked up to the children, waved, then saddled his pack across his back and trudged down the canyon, disappearing from sight.

Little Fox waited until he was certain the trader was gone, that he would not return. Then he turned back toward the village where his mother was preparing the early morning meal. Brown-skinned children were running and shouting to each other as the village came to life with a great deal of noise and confusion. Dogs of all sizes were barking while turkeys strutted from their roosts in the back of the cave.

Little Fox could not imagine living in houses that could be carried on one's back. He had always lived in this village. The one-room, stone houses filled the cave end to end. Each house had a rectangular or T-shaped door but no windows. The houses were built in terraces. Some were only one story high while others reached the arching roof of the cave. Ladders led from one level to another. There were both round and square houses, some as high as four stories. The stone courtyard was located in front of the village. There smoke from the many fires was curling toward the roof of the cave. Smoke was also coming from several openings in the floor of the courtyard.

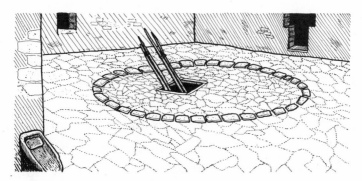

Running Deer came up behind Little Fox, pointing to the ladders leading to the underground ceremonial chambers, called kivas, and said, "Next spring, you know, we will be old enough to learn the secrets of the kivas." Little Fox wondered if the ladders were beckoning in, or offering a quick way out if one needed to leave in a hurry. Running Deer, who often sat and stared at the ladders because they offered a way into the kivas, sighed. "I wish I were already twelve, or would be this year."

"You are in too big a hurry to grow up," Little Fox replied. "We must wait our time." He watched his father, Eagle Hunter, climb out of one of the kiva openings. He wore only a loin-cloth fastened around his short, stocky body. His dark brown hair was tied in two knots at the back, one on top of the other. A necklace of greenish-blue stone hung around his thick muscular neck. He moved gracefully toward their home.

Little Fox's mother, White Flower, motioned to him. Leaving Running Deer looking wistfully at the ladders, Little Fox ran to her. "The meal is ready," she said as Little Fox sat down. Her round, pleasant face glowed from the warmth of the fire. The red feather pendant around her neck swayed as she moved the steaming pot from the fire to the center of the family group. All eyes except grandfather's sightless ones were on the pot. Straggly white hair stuck out around his wrinkled face, contrasting with the dark brown face of Butterfly Girl, who sat next to him. She and Little Fox looked very much alike, with the same haircut and the same bright dark eyes watching the pot of food. She leaned against the woven cotton blanket grandfather had wrapped around him and said, "I'm hungry."

Laughing, Eagle Hunter replied, "You are always hungry." Then his broad face became serious. "We must not forget the gods." He took a pinch of the savory deer stew from the white clay pot. The black design on its sides seemed to grow darker as Eagle Hunter threw the small portion of food into the fire. He did the same with the cornbread. "Now the gods will be kind to this family."

Using their fingers, the family members dipped their cornbread into the stew. Little Fox glanced across the fire at his older sister, Blue Bird. Though her soft brown eyes were serious, her pretty face broke into a smile when she saw Little Fox looking at her.

"What is it you wish to know, little one?" she asked.

"I am not little," Little Fox replied, solemnly. "I wish to know if it is true that you will soon marry?"

"Yes," she answered. "I am of age now and the

agreement has been made."

"That is soon," White Flower said. "Today is now and today Blue Bird and I will hunt for greens. They should be easy to find after the warm sunshine of the past few days." The tender green shoots of many plants were a special treat for the family.

"A change from dried meat and cornmeal will be welcome," commented Eagle Hunter. He turned to Little Fox. "Today we must start clearing the cornfields. It will not be long before the signs will be right for the planting."

The meal finished, Little Fox picked up a stick with a sharp chisel-like stone blade attached and started across the courtyard.

His dog yawned, stretched his brown and black body, and followed.

At the edge of the village, Running Deer was waiting, a frown on his light brown face. "My father says I must help too," he said. "It is such hard work."

"This is not a time to be lazy, Running Deer," Little Fox said. "You know how important clearing the fields is to our people."

Running Deer nodded his head in agreement, eyes cast downward as he trailed along behind Little Fox. They left the village and began the climb to the mesa above. Running Deer led, using the hand and toe notches cut into the

rock face. He climbed like a mountain sheep,
quickly and surely. Little Fox followed close
behind. He liked the feel of the warm rock beneath his fingers and bare toes. A large shadow
glided over the rock face. He looked up just in
time to see an eagle soar out over the canyon.
He knew the eagle was a good sign.

As Little Fox reached the flat land of the
mesa, Dog came bounding up. He had found his
own way to the mesa top. Everywhere Little
Fox looked, he could see the men and boys of
the village at work digging up dead rabbit brush
and yucca roots from the cornfields. Some men
were beginning to clear new fields. He could
hear the dull thud of stone axes against tree

trunks. The air was heavy with the scent of juniper and pinyon pine. Many brush piles were already burning, sending columns of smoke toward the clear blue sky.

Little Fox and Running Deer started working in their clan's field. The dark red soil came up rich and soft under their stone hoes and the sun felt warmly good on their bare backs. Having discarded their blankets, they wore only loincloths fastened around their waists.

All morning they worked, stopping just long enough to eat some cornbread from the deerskin pouches they carried. Later in the afternoon, Butterfly Girl brought them cool water in a black and white clay jar. As the sun lowered in the western sky, the men and boys started back to the village.

"I will race you to the edge of the cliff," Running Deer called to Little Fox, who leaned his hoe against a juniper tree and started to run. Running Deer was always challenging him to a footrace. Maybe that was because Running Deer knew he could always win, because he was taller and had longer legs. Little Fox liked to race, even if he did feel tired from the day's work, so he ran with zest and vigor. Both boys reached the edge of the cliff out of breath, and Little Fox was surprised that he had run as close to Running Deer as he had. He called Dog as Running Deer started down the cliff. "Here, Dog. Come, Dog," he called several times but he could not see the dog anywhere. Just a short time ago, he had been chasing a squirrel. Just then, Little Fox heard Dog barking. Though he knew he should go on to the village, he was curious about Dog's barking. He ran along the edge of the mesa in the direction of the noise. Climbing over some rocks he could see Dog standing on a ledge, at the opening of a small cave. He was barking at something inside. Little Fox crept closer, his heart beating rapidly. The opening of the cave loomed ever larger and more darkly before him. He could hear a rustling inside.

· Chapter II ·
Little Fox Makes
a Discovery

Moving still closer to the cave, Little Fox peered into the darkness. Could it be a mountain lion that had attracted Dog's attention?

Suddenly, an object came hurtling out of the cave, hitting Little Fox in the stomach and knocking him flat, close to the edge of the band of rock jutting out in front of the cave. He had only a second to see that the object was a person and not an animal before he was forced to defend himself against a pair of flying fists. Quickly, Little Fox rolled over and pinned his opponent's arms to the ground.

"Stop fighting," he said, as he looked into the brown eyes of a boy about his own age. "I am not going to hurt you."

At the sound of Little Fox's voice, the boy stopped struggling. Little Fox could feel the boy's ribs through his garment. His face was drawn and gaunt. He looked as if he had not eaten for a long time. Slowly, Little Fox got up. He opened his pouch, which had fallen on the ground during the struggle, and took out a piece of cornbread. He extended the bread toward the boy who eagerly grabbed it and gulped it down.

Little Fox laughed. "You act just like Dog when he is hungry," he said, but the boy's attention was on the food. While the boy ate, Little Fox had a chance to look closely at him. He had a slim, brown face with high cheek bones and an angular chin. His shiny black hair was longer than Little Fox's and was tied into bunches on each side of his head with leather thongs. When he turned, Little Fox could see that the boy's head was round in back and not flat like his own. A tremor ran up his spine, settling at the base of his head and making the fine hairs stand out from his neck and scalp. He knew that this boy was one of the strangers that the old trader had talked about. What he did not know was whether the boy was of a friendly tribe that perhaps traded with his own people or if he came from a people who made war. His leggings and tunic-type of shirt were made of animal skin, and much different from the clothes Little Fox wore. Though he knew it was rude to do so, Little Fox could not stop staring at the boy. Finally, his curiosity prompted him to ask the boy where he came from. No response. He said, "I am Little Fox," and he pointed to himself. Then he pointed to the boy. "What is your name? Can you tell me your name?"

This time, the boy seemed to understand. He pointed to Little Fox and said, "Little Fox." Then he pointed to himself and said, "Judi Yezzi."

"I do not understand," Little Fox said. He looked at the strange boy closely. "He really looks like I should look," he thought. "He is lean and angular, like the fox. But I am Little Fox. I should be named for the owl, like those in this cave where I found him, but I cannot have that name. I know, I will give that name to him, so that he can be my friend." He moved toward the boy, and touched him on the arm, pointing toward himself first and saying, "Little Fox." Then he touched the boy on the chest and said, "Gray Owl. You are Gray Owl." The boy smiled, nodded, touched himself and repeated, "Gray Owl."

Little Fox touched Gray Owl once more, then pointed in several different directions while asking, "Where do you come from? Where do you live? How did you get here?" Gray Owl nodded again, picked up a stick and began to make marks on the cave floor, in the soft dirt. Little Fox watched him draw a mountain. Below the mountain, Gray Owl drew the figure of a man with a pack on his back. Behind the man, he drew a smaller figure.

Little Fox had seen the trader draw like that. The trader! The figure with the pack! Then Gray Owl must be the smaller figure. He had done what Little Fox had wanted to do: Gray Owl had followed the trader from the mountains up the canyon to the mesa country. Little Fox thought, "Gray Owl must be from the wandering tribes who have been raiding the villages of my people. He is an enemy! But he does not look like an enemy. And he does not act like an enemy. And he is just a boy like myself. Then he must be from a tribe that trades with my people. He must be a friend!" Having settled the matter to his own satisfaction, Little Fox suddenly noticed that darkness was closing around them. He would have to get back to the village or his family would come looking for him. Little Fox thought to himself: "What am I going to do? He is my friend but my people will think that he is an enemy and they will not let him come into the village, even if he is only a small boy! I cannot take him with me; I must keep him hidden."

With hand signals, gestures and much pointing, Little Fox made it somewhat clear that he would have to return to the village, but that he would return when he could—with food. Gray Owl nodded his agreement, curled into a circle, and fell asleep.

Little Fox climbed down the cliff and entered the village where fires for the evening meal were burning and families were gathering for the evening meal. Shadows danced on the dark, golden stone houses. He hurried on to his own family fire. His mother was setting out a pot of deer stew and a pot of the green sprouts she and Blue Bird had gathered that day. Little Fox's mouth began to water when he smelled the wild onion seasoning. His father looked at him as he sat down in the family circle.

"Where have you been, Little Fox?" His father asked.

"Dog was barking at something and I went to see what it was," he replied, hoping his father would not ask any more questions. Little Fox had never lied to his father before, and he could not lie easily nor well. To his relief, his father turned his attention to the ceremony for the evening meal. He threw a pinch of food from each pot into the fire.

As each member of the family took a portion from the cooking pots, Little Fox breathed easier. It was obvious they were interested in eating and not in what he had been doing. He was just beginning to relax when Butterfly Girl said, "Father, the trader told us about the people of the mountains. Will they come here? Will they hurt us? I am afraid."

"Do not worry, Butterfly Girl, we are in a safe place. They will not come here," her father assured her.

Then Grandfather raised his head and began to speak. "Remember the trading party which never returned to the village last spring? Some say the mountain people killed them. They are our enemies." That said, the old man's head sank low on his chest, as if talking were a great effort. In the silence that followed, Little Fox gazed into the fire.

"A small boy is not the enemy," he thought. "If I ran away to follow the trader and went to his family, I would not be the enemy either. He is in the cave, all alone, and is probably very hungry. There was not much food in the pouch. Poor little Gray Owl, he is my friend and I must help him."

The village began to settle for the night. The men and boys went down the ladders into the kivas. The women and children spread out their mats of animal skins in the houses and crawled into their warm blankets. Little Fox lay in his blanket in the small room he shared with his mother and sisters. He could not get his mind off Gray Owl. He listened as the village slowly became quiet.

When he thought everyone was asleep, he rose from his mat, pulled his blanket around him, and crept out to the low burning fire. He took a clay bowl and filled it with stew. Moving very slowly, he crept past the silent houses. The flickering fires had burned low, but they still lighted his way. Dog came to join him and together they moved away from the sleeping people. As Little Fox started up the cliff, Dog ran toward his own route, eagerly.

The night was dark, with only a sliver of moon in the star-sprinkled sky, but the way was familiar to his feet. Then Little Fox jerked to a stop, heart hammering, at an eerie cry sailing from across the canyon. "Ho, that was the call of a fox," he said with a shaky laugh, embarrassed at his unease. "He will not hurt me." He had at first thought the call to be that of a witch. He knew they came out at night and caused illness among his people. His legs shook at the thought of meeting one, but he thought he could not allow himself to be afraid. The boy, Gray Owl, needed food. "Besides," he thought, as Dog ran to meet him at the top of the mesa, "Dog is with me and he is not afraid of anything—not even witches."

· Chapter III ·
The Secret

Little Fox felt secure as he rested his hand on the strong back of Dog. They carefully made their way through the darkness to the opening of the cave. Under the overhang, Gray Owl had built a small fire which Little Fox had not been able to see from above. Gray Owl was sitting huddled close to the fire, his tunic pulled tightly around him. He leaped up when Little Fox came near, then smiled when he saw who had made the noise.

"I have brought you some food," Little Fox said, shoving the bowl of stew toward Gray Owl. With a nod, the boy took the bowl and began to eat. When he had finished, he put his hand on Little Fox's shoulder. They looked at each other and smiled. Little Fox turned and started back toward home, not wanting his family to find him gone.

For many days, Little Fox kept his secret. He was afraid to tell anyone about the boy in the cave. He knew what bitter enmity existed between his people and the mountain people and he had seen that hostility worked out against captives. He wondered what his people would do if they found out about Gray Owl and shuddered to think of the possibilities. Each day he managed to find time to visit the cave and take food to his new friend. Little Fox also taught Gray Owl to speak the language of his people and they spent hours sitting in the warm sunshine, talking. Each day, their friendship grew.

Little Fox found it hard to be with Gray Owl and still help in the fields. One day, as he was working with the men and boys, Running Deer came up to him.

"Where have you been going each day, Little Fox? Many times I have looked for you and I could not find you."

Little Fox dropped his head. He had been avoiding Running Deer, not wanting him to learn the secret of Gray Owl. He kept his eyes on the ground and dug furiously with his stone hoe. "I have been here and there," he mumbled. Running Deer looked at him impatiently then trotted off to another field when Little Fox would say no more. Running Deer was getting suspicious, Little Fox knew.

While the fields were being prepared for the corn, beans, and squash, the weather was getting warmer. The priests had been watching the signs in the activities of the animals and birds. They noted every type of plant that appeared. It was important to plant the corn at the right time. The moon was watched. The corn must be planted as the moon was growing so that the corn would grow with it. It must be planted just before the spring rains started. The priests must watch for the signs of the coming rain.

One night just as the evening meal was ending, the Crier Chief climbed the ladder to a low roof in the center of the village. The people became quiet and listened for his announcement.

"People of the village, Sun Watcher tells me all the signs are right for the ceremonial planting of the corn tomorrow," he shouted. Excited voices broke out all over the village. The long awaited day had come.

Little Fox's family got up at first light. Little Fox watched his father put a small amount of corn into a special pouch made from the entire skin of a fawn. He knew that as a fawn grows, the corn would grow. White Flower poured water over Eagle Hunter as he got ready to leave the village. She said, "This water represents the rains that will come to make the corn grow."

When the rituals had been completed, Little Fox followed his father up the cliff to the fields. Then, in the center of the field, Eagle Hunter dug four holes, one to the north, one to the west, one to the south, and one to the east. Two more holes were dug, one close to the north hole, and the other close to the south hole. Kneeling and saying a prayer, he placed a plumed prayer stick in the center of a cross he made of cornmeal. He also sprinkled the prayer stick with cornmeal. Next, he selected four corn grains of each color. He knelt in the center and dropped the yellow kernels into the north hole as he chanted a prayer. Continuing the chant, he dropped the blue grains into the west hole, the red corn into the south hole, and the white into the east hole. The speckled and black kernels were placed in the two remaining holes.

All of the holes were then filled with soil. Next Eagle Hunter planted four long rows of corn. Each row started at the center plot and radiated out toward the four directions.

With this ceremony to insure bountiful corn crops, the planting for the first day was over. Little Fox and his family had to wait four days before the rest of the fields could be planted. During these four days, Eagle Hunter performed many ceremonial rituals.

On the fifth day, Little Fox and his father rose early to start planting the remaining corn.

"Hurry, Little Fox, we must get all the fields planted before the rains come," Eagle Hunter said as they gathered up the pouches of seed. "Butterfly Girl and Blue Bird must come with us and help. Your mother will bring us water."

The mesa top was a place of frenzied activity for the next few days as the corn, beans and squash were planted. Finally one evening, the last seed was dropped into the last hole and tamped down with a brown foot. All stood quietly, aware of the large black cloud that had been forming over the distant horizon. Judging by the moist and heavy air, rain would soon fall.

There were smiles on the faces of Little Fox's family as they gathered up the empty seed pouches and water jars. Happily, they started toward the edge of the canyon and the trail down.

"I will come later," Little Fox called to his mother as she started down the cliff.

"Do not be long," she answered. "The evening meal will be ready soon."

With Dog at his heels, Little Fox started off along the canyon rim. He was hoping Gray Owl had not been too lonesome—or too hungry—for the past few days.

"Gray Owl," he called as he neared the cave.

"I am here, Little Fox," Gray Owl answered.

Little Fox thought Gray Owl sounded like one of his own people, he had learned so much in the short time that Little Fox had been teaching him.

Just then, they heard a noise from the direction Little Fox had taken to the cave.

A familiar voice called out, "Little Fox, where are you?"

"That is Running Deer," Little Fox said. "Quick! Hide in the cave!"

But it was too late. Running Deer had already seen Gray Owl. He stopped short.

"Who is that, Little Fox?" he asked in a puzzled voice, pointing to Gray Owl.

"This is my friend Gray Owl." replied Little Fox. "He has been staying in this cave."

"What is he doing here? He does not look like our people," Running Deer looked at Gray Owl accusingly.

"He followed the trader here from the mountains," Little Fox explained. "The trader told him many stories about the people who live in the great stone cities on the mesa. He wanted to see them for himself. He did not know it would be so far and he cannot find his way back. I found him and fed him and we have become friends."

"No!" Running Deer shouted. "He cannot be

your friend! He is an enemy," he was slowly
backing away from Gray Owl, watching him
closely. "I will tell our people about this enemy!"
He turned and quickly scrambled over the
rocks toward the cliff face.

· Chapter IV ·
The Council's Decision

"Little Fox, what will they do, when Running Deer tells the people of your village about me?" asked Gray Owl. The fear he felt showed in his eyes.

"I do not know," Little Fox replied. "But I am your friend. I will help you."

They did not have long to wait. Soon they heard angry voices coming their way. It seemed as if all the people of the village were coming along the canyon rim. The Village Chief was leading the group, followed closely by the other members of the council. Eagle Hunter was also there.

"Little Fox, what have you done?" asked the Village Chief. His voice was angry, and his wide brown face was set in stern lines.

"This is Gray Owl," Little Fox said, pointing to his friend. "He has been staying in this cave. He has not caused any harm to anyone."

"Running Deer says he comes from the mountain people," the Chief said. "Is that true?"

"Yes," Little Fox replied, "but he is not an

enemy. He is my friend."

"Come, we will go to the village and the Council will decide what will be done about the boy," the Village Chief said. He took Gray Owl by the arm and started toward the canyon rim.

Little Fox fell into step with his father, behind the Chief and Gray Owl. "I am sorry if I have caused trouble," he said, "but he was so hungry and lost I could not leave him to find his way home. I took him food and water and taught him our language so that we could speak together. Now he is my friend." He looked at his father's face and could see that there was no use in his talking. He remained silent as he followed with the group to the village.

When they came to the edge of the cliff and started down the hand-and-toe notches, Little Fox saw Gray Owl draw back in terror. The Chief tugged his arm, but Gray Owl could only stare over the side of the cliff in shock and horror.

"Come, boy, what is the matter with you?" asked the Chief.

"I cannot climb down there," Gray Owl said in a quivering voice. He was shaking all over.

Little Fox could see that Gray Owl feared the steep descent they had to make to reach the village.

"Father, please help him," Little Fox pleaded. "He is not used to this kind of climb, even

though he is as old as I am."

Eagle Hunter started forward after he looked intently at Little Fox, searching his face. He pushed his way through the crowd. "Here, boy," he said to Gray Owl. "Climb onto my back." Still shaking, Gray Owl put his arms around Eagle Hunter's neck. His eyes were closed tightly when Eagle Hunter turned his broad back to the canyon, felt with his toes for the first notch, and started down. With ease he descended the cliff and deposited Gray Owl at the bottom. As he was being led toward the village, Gray Owl glanced up with a shudder at the cliff they had just come down.

When the group came in sight of the village, Gray Owl stopped short. His eyes were big and round as he stared in amazement. "I have never seen anything like it," Gray Owl said in awe. "The trader described it, but I did not know it would be so big! And houses of stone!"

The Village Chief announced that all would eat first and then talk. "Our people have worked hard today, and are hungry," he concluded.

With that, the people scattered to their own fires.

Little Fox led Gray Owl to his own family. His mother lifted a large, corrugated pot off the fire. The usual comments preceding the meal were absent, as all ate in silence. Little Fox saw the hostile glances directed toward Gray Owl. The silence continued until the Chief came to get Gray Owl, who was led toward the circle of men sitting in the center of the village. Little Fox followed at a short distance to a point from which he could see the stern faces of the Council as they watched the strange boy approaching. "What will they do?" Little Fox wondered worriedly.

The Village Chief began to question Gray Owl. "Why did you come to our mesa?" he asked.

"The trader told me about the stone villages. I wanted to see them for myself."

"Will your people come looking for you?" asked the Chief.

"No, I do not think they will," Gray Owl replied. "My parents were killed by other people from the north. I have no one who cares for me except my grandfather, who is very old."

A man Little Fox recognized, from a village farther down the canyon, said something to the Chief. They had a brief discussion in low tones. Little Fox could not hear what they were saying.

The Chief came over to stand in front of Gray Owl. He said, "Go with Little Fox to his family. We will now make our decision."

Little Fox and Gray Owl sat in front of the fire and watched the circle of men. They were arguing. Sometimes their voices became loud enough to hear a word or two. Once, one of the village leaders leaped up, gestured with his arms and shouted something. Others nodded in approval. Little Fox saw his father stand and talk quietly, looking at each man in turn. Finally, after what seemed to be a long time, the Village Chief motioned for Gray Owl to come to the center of the circle.

"A trader from another village has told us that your people have left the flat land and have moved back to the mountains," he said. "We do not think they will try to find you. Since the old trader knows your people, we will wait until he returns to learn more about their movements. You will stay with Little Fox's family. Eagle Hunter is willing to take responsibility for you."

"Come," Eagle Hunter said, "it is late. We will go to bed." He led Gray Owl toward their house. Little Fox followed, thinking of all the decisions that could have been made, the bad along with this good one.

"Thank you, father," Little Fox said. "Gray Owl will not be any trouble to you."

"See that he is not," his father remarked with a stern look at the two boys.

The next morning, Little Fox awoke to the soft patter of rain. He lay in his blanket and thought about Gray Owl sleeping beside him.

He must help his friend learn the ways of his people who—he was sure—would accept the strange boy who was his friend.

Chatter around the morning fires focused on two events: the coming of the spring rains and the coming of the boy called Gray Owl.

"We will have water for making pots now," White Flower was saying to Blue Bird when Little Fox and Gray Owl joined the family. "We must make some large ones to hold the water we will need this summer."

"Little Fox, we will check the dams in the canyon to see that they will hold the heavy run-off water," Eagle Hunter said. "Gray Owl must help too."

Later, as the two boys started down over the refuse heap in the front of the village, a group of children came running up to them. Running Deer was in the lead.

"Little Fox, you are not taking him, are you?" he asked, pointing at Gray Owl.

"Gray Owl will help me with the dams," Little Fox said.

"But I always help you," Running Deer complained.

"Come with us if you want to," Little Fox invited.

But Running Deer only laughed, nodding at Gray Owl. "He is afraid of the cliffs and besides, he looks funny. He does not look like our people. He has a round head."

The other children in the group started laughing. Some of the smaller ones began dancing around Gray Owl, chanting, "Round, round, round head."

Gray Owl stared over their heads as if he did not hear them, immobile until Little Fox took his arm, urging him away from the group of children. "Come, Gray Owl, we must check the dams," he said.

• Chapter V •
Gray Owl Learns About Village Life

In the canyon below the village, Little Fox showed Gray Owl how the stones should be placed in the wall of a dam so the water would not leak out. They did not mind the warm gentle rain that was falling on their bare backs. The precious water was running down the sides of the canyon in small streams. It was beginning to collect in pools behind the stone and earth dams. Other boys from the village were repairing some of the dams, but they stayed away from Little Fox and Gray Owl, as if they were afraid Gray Owl would hurt them in some way.

When the boys returned to the village, White Flower and Butterfly Girl were busy working over a lump of blue-gray clay.

"What are they doing?" Gray Owl asked, sitting on a stone wall near them.

"They are getting ready to make pottery," Little Fox replied. "They dug the clay from the bed at the head of the canyon."

White Flower looked up from her work and smiled at them. "I have worked in the fine powder made from grinding down the broken

pottery pieces," she explained to Gray Owl. "We use it to keep the pot from shrinking or cracking as it dries. We have added water to give it just the right thickness."

"What will you do now?" asked Gray Owl.

"Just watch and see," White Flower replied, as she pinched off a small piece of clay from the large heap.

She laid it on a smooth stone and rolled it with the palm of her hand. A long, round rope of clay began to form from the shapeless mass. After she had made several round ropes, she began to coil one of them around and around on itself. Each time a coil was added, she pinched the edges together.

"I am making a large water jar," she explained. "It will take many clay ropes."

Little Fox and Gray Owl could see the jar taking shape as she worked. When she had the coils in place, she began to smooth the outside and inside of the jar.

"The shape must be just right," White Flower said, stopping to look at her jar with a critical eye. "See, there is a small bulge on the side." Her brown fingers moved rapidly and the bulge disappeared.

Little Fox turned to look at Butterfly Girl's bowl. Her coils were uneven, fat in some places and thin in others. The bowl was leaning to one side.

"Look at Butterfly Girl's bowl," he said, laughing. "It looks like it is going to fall over."

"Do not pay any attention to him, Butterfly Girl," her mother said. "You will learn how to make beautiful pottery."

"What do you do to the jar now?" asked Gray Owl, who was still interested in the process of making pottery.

"After it dries in the sun, I will cover it with a thin, white clay and polish it with a smooth pebble," explained White Flower. "Then, I will paint a design on it with a thick, brown liquid made from boiling the shoots of the beeweed plant. The final step will be firing it in that shallow pit over there." She pointed to a hole close by. "I will cover it with wood and bark. The fire will get very hot and the jar will become hard. The brown paint of the design will turn to a deep black."

Gray Owl looked around at the women of the village, all engaged in making pottery. Many shapes and sizes of finished and unfinished clay pots displayed their art.

"My people do not make pottery, though I think it would be good for them to learn," Gray Owl said to Little Fox. He sighed and stared out over the canyon. Little Fox wondered if he were thinking of the life he had left behind.

Then the warm rainy days slid by swiftly for Little Fox and Gray Owl. The new boy was interested in all the activities of the village people, but he could not be persuaded to go to the mesa top with Little Fox and Running Deer who went each day to inspect the tiny green shoots which were pushing up through the rich red soil of the cornfields.

The spring rains were also necessary for the growth of the wild plants that were so important to the people of the mesa. The stalks of the yucca plants thrust their waxy, white bell-shaped flowers toward the sky. Down close to the ground, the prickly pear cactus was spreading its yellow flowers. Both of these plants would produce a fruit that would be gathered and eaten in the fall. With the wonders of spring, the dangers and fears of the past seemed far behind them. There seemed to be no flaw, no problem in the life they were living.

Then, one day Eagle Hunter called to them. "We must gather stones for the house Bluebird and her husband will move into when they are married. It will be built next to White Flower's House."

"Why there?" Gray Owl asked as they started toward the canyon.

"The women of the village own the houses," Eagle Hunter explained. "When a girl marries, her new husband moves in with her family. He must learn to live with his in-laws, which is not always easy. However, he goes back to his own family's kiva for ceremonies, and also to visit." He paused. "We keep the customs of the past that are good customs, and this one seems to be very good."

After the boys had collected a large pile of stones, they made a sling of deerskin to carry the stones to the village. Other members of the clan were also collecting rocks. When Little Fox saw Running Deer carrying a large stone to the village, he ran to him, saying, "Let me help you, Running Deer."

"No," Running Deer frowned. "I can do it

myself." He pulled away from Little Fox, lurching under the weight of the rock.

Little Fox watched him, puzzled. Why was Running Deer acting so strangely? And this was not the first time that he had been rude and withdrawn. Little Fox shrugged, then turned back to his own work.

When a large pile of stones had been carried to the spot where the new house was to be built, the men of the clan began to chip the edges of the stones. The sandstone was fairly soft. In a short time the stone hammers could shape the odd-sized stones into building blocks. The pecking sound of stone on stone could be heard all over the village.

Several houses were being built or repaired that spring.

As Gray Owl watched the skillful fingers of the men shape the stones, he asked, "Little Fox, how do they get the stones to stay together when they start to build the walls?"

Little Fox pointed to where his mother was stirring a pot of gray clay. "Mother is making a mixture of clay and water that will be spread between the stones. When it hardens, it will hold the stones in place."

For the next few days, Gray Owl watched with interest as the house took shape. It was small, so the work went fast. Blue Bird was the center of much teasing and laughing as the work progressed.

As soon as the walls were a little taller than Blue Bird, the men placed heavy poles across the walls. Over these, they spread a layer of straight, round sticks. Next came a covering of bark, followed by a thick adobe roof. When this was done, Blue Bird spread a thin coat of white plaster over the inside walls. She also painted some designs on the walls. She smiled as she worked, the pride in her new house showing in her soft brown eyes. This small room would be home to her for the rest of her life. It would hold herself, her husband, and any children they might have, as well as the few possessions they had acquired for their life together.

Now that the house for Blue Bird had been completed, the men of the clan turned their attention to the fields on the mesa. Little Fox knew he and Gray Owl would be expected to help in the fields.

One morning after the rains had stopped and the sun had come out, Little Fox took Gray Owl to the foot of the cliff.

"Come, Gray Owl, you must learn to climb to the mesa. I will show you how."

· Chapter VI ·
The Unattended Field

Gray Owl hung back as they neared the base of the sheer rock wall. Little Fox pushed him forward with a firm hand in his back.

"Watch carefully while I climb," he said. He placed his toes in the first notch and reached for the next one with his fingers. Slowly, to illustrate each step, he climbed. He glanced back over his shoulder at the frightened boy on the ground.

"You must always start with the right foot or you will get stuck half way up," he shouted, as he reached the top. "Now try it," he coaxed.

Gray Owl had already climbed the shorter cliff to the canyon floor, so he was not as terrified as he had been before. But the lower cliff was not this far above the canyon floor.

Just as he was putting his foot into the first notch, Running Deer came up behind him.

"Are you afraid to climb?" he asked. He began to laugh.

Little Fox saw the determined look on Gray Owl's slim face as he started to climb. His hair swung from side to side. Maybe the teasing helped after all, he thought.

When Gray Owl reached the top, he had a big smile on his face. His brown eyes sparkling, he looked as if he had just killed the first deer of the hunt.

That day, the boys worked hard in the fields. The sun was warm, but a cool breeze blew over the mesa. It ruffled their hair and cooled their faces as they worked. Weeds had come up with the corn, beans and squash. They had to be carefully chopped out to avoid hurting the tiny sprouts that had come up everywhere. Once Little Fox's hoe dislodged a large lizard from a rock where it had been sunning itself. The boys laughed when it reared up on its hind legs and scampered away. The black band around its neck stood out against its scaly, green body.

The men and boys of the village loved their fields and spent most of their time there as the days passed. The corn was growing tall and straight. If nothing happened, they would have a good crop. They worked all morning in the fields, but as the days became warmer, the afternoons were spent in the shade of the juniper and pinyon pine trees. There was plenty to do, even in the hot part of the day.

"Here, Gray Owl, let me show you how to fasten the stone to the stick," Little Fox said, when he saw his friend trying to make a digging stick.

"When I learn this, I want to see if I can make a pair of yucca-fiber sandals like your people wear," Gray Owl said.

They were sitting in the shade of a juniper tree after a morning of hoeing corn. All around them, the men were busy at a variety of tasks. One man was repairing his broken bow while another was straightening an arrow by pulling it through a slot in a stone. Dog was lying in the dry soil, his tongue lolling out the side of his mouth. Eagle Hunter was sitting nearby working on a bone necklace.

"Little Fox, it will be your turn to watch this field for the next few days," he said, looking at the two boys who were sitting with their heads together. They were just finishing the digging stick.

"Yes, Father, we will start tonight," Little Fox replied. He knew the fields were never left unattended. The men and boys took turns watching them.

"Running Deer will help too," Eagle Hunter said. "It will take all three of you to keep the animals and birds from destroying the crops. You can sleep in the brush shelter which I have built."

That night, the three boys built a fire and roasted the rabbit they had killed near the field earlier in the day. Running Deer sat as far away from the other two boys as he could and still be within the circle of firelight. Little Fox could tell he was afraid of the witches who wandered at night, but he did not want to be close to Gray Owl. Before long, the three boys, tired from their work in the fields, were asleep in the brush shelter.

The next morning, Running Deer seemed in a better mood.

"I will race you to the old dead tree over that ridge," he said to Little Fox.

"We must not leave the fields," Little Fox reminded him.

"Are you afraid I will beat you again?" Running Deer asked. He looked at Little Fox's short legs and stocky body. He laughed.

"You might beat me, but you can not beat Gray Owl," Little Fox said angrily.

"I will show you," Running Deer cried. He

started to run, followed closely by the other two boys. Dog raced along yipping at their heels.

Little Fox and Gray Owl stayed close to Running Deer as they ran swiftly through the trees. They reached the old tree with Gray Owl and Running Deer running side by side. Little Fox brought up the rear. They dropped to the ground out of breath.

Running Deer frowned at Gray Owl. "I will beat you next time," he said between gasps for air.

They sat for a few minutes under the old tree before starting back toward the field. As they neared the shelter, they heard a thrashing noise ahead of them. A herd of deer leaped through the brush, their white tails waving, the boys started to run.

"Look at the cornfield," Little Fox cried.

What the deer had not eaten of the tender stalks, they had trampled under their sharp hooves. The bean plants and squash vines were pulled up and scattered around. The tiny, new vegetables were smashed. It did not look like there was one stalk of corn left in the entire field.

"We are in trouble, and it is all your fault." Running Deer accused, turning to Gray Owl.

"How can you blame him?" Little Fox asked in a shocked voice. "We were all to blame."

"He did not have to race with us," Running

Deer mumbled. "He should have stayed to watch the field."

"What will your father do to us?" asked Gray Owl in a small voice.

"I do not know," Little Fox replied, "but we will soon find out. I hear someone coming."

As the boys feared, Eagle Hunter was coming toward them. They hung their heads guiltily as he looked at the shambles of the cornpatch where green stalks had once grown.

"What has happened to the corn?" Eagle Hunter asked. "I can see the deer tracks. How could this happen with you watching it?"

"We left for only a short time," Little Fox tried to explain.

"Gray Owl could have stayed to watch the corn," Running Deer said.

"All three of you should have stayed close," said Eagle Hunter. "Come with me."

· Chapter VII ·
The
Summer Storm

Eagle Hunter started back toward the village. The three boys followed silently. Little Fox was wondering what kind of punishment his father had in mind. He knew that they deserved to be punished, and severely. He had known from the time that he was first put to work in the fields that the corn was the most important aspect of his village: it meant life or death to his clan. The only redeeming consideration was that there were other fields and, if the harvest were good, they might be able to do without this one and its loss would not seem so serious as it now appeared.

When they reached the village, Eagle Hunter led the three boys to the stone wall where Grandfather sat hunched in his blanket. Eagle Hunter explained the situation to the old man. Grandfather's brown and withered face was sad and serious as he started to talk to the boys. Little Fox sat down on the cold stones of the courtyard. He knew this lecture would take a long time.

A group of children began to gather as the old, blind man talked on and on about the importance of responsibility and the importance of the corn in their lives. The three boys began to squirm as all eyes were upon them. A lecture from an older person was the most dreaded of all punishments. The children knew that they would have to bear the humiliation of everyone knowing that they had failed to meet their responsibility, even though no one would ever again speak of the matter. They also knew that they would never again leave the fields unattended.

Little Fox, Gray Owl, and Running Deer were the topic of talk for several days, though no one spoke to them directly about the matter. Then the interest of the clan turned to the coming marriage of Blue Bird.

Gray Owl watched the bustle and excitement of Little Fox's family over the approaching marriage.

"Who is Blue Bird going to marry?" he asked Little Fox.

"A boy from a clan on the other side of the village. He sent his mother to my family to arrange the marriage," explained Little Fox. "They agreed on the gifts which will be exchanged."

"Does Blue Bird want to marry him?" Gray Owl asked.

"Yes, she agreed. Before you came to the village, she went to the boy's house for four days, all the women of his clan inspected her work and were pleased."

"Now that my clan has built their house, the marriage will take place," Little Fox told his friend.

Soon the boy from the other side of the village arrived with his clothing, weapons and tools. After the wedding ceremony and feast, they moved into the house built for them.

That evening around the fire, the family admired the shell necklace that Blue Bird had received from her new husband.

"You must have had something valuable to trade to get those shells," Butterfly Girl said to the young man.

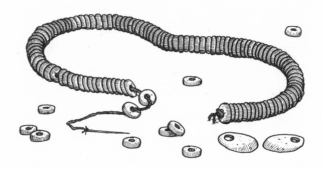

"Hush, Butterfly Girl," her mother said, smiling at the young couple. "The marriage has come at a good time," she continued. "We will have more room in our house for our new baby who will come in the fall."

"I do not need another sister," said Little Fox, making a face at Butterfly Girl.

"We shall see," White Flower said, laughing at them. "Now that Blue Bird is married and the corn is coming along well, you must spend more time learning the traditions of our people," she said to Little Fox.

"Will Gray Owl be able to learn too?" asked Little Fox.

White Flower thought for a while. "That will be up to your uncle," she said. "He will be the one teaching you, but I do not think my brother will mind."

Little Fox turned to explain to Gray Owl. "My mother's oldest brother is my 'ceremonial father.' He is responsible for all my training. I must be ready to enter the society of the kiva next spring."

For several days after that, the boys spent the hot afternoons sitting in the shade of a tree listening to Little Fox's uncle. He told them that their people believe the sun is their father and the earth is their mother. The people came into being in a dark cave in the center of the earth. As time passed, they climbed into caves with more light. Finally, they climbed up through a hole in the earth called the sipapu. All other creatures came to this world by the same route. Each kiva has a small, plug-filled hole in the bottom of it which represents the original sipapu.

One day while the boys were having their instruction, Eagle Hunter came running from the village.

"The Hunt Chief has been shot," he said excitedly. "The arrow has gone through his leg. The medicine man is going to perform a healing ceremony."

As they entered the village, they noticed the increased activity of the people. Little Fox and Gray Owl watched as the head medicine man rushed past them toward the house of the Hunt

Chief where others were silently gathering. Then, the medicine man began his healing chants. Before long someone was sent to bring other medicine men. It must be a serious wound, Little Fox thought, as the men pushed through the crowd that waited patiently for news.

An old man limped up to Eagle Hunter.

"How did it happen?" he asked in a hoarse voice. "Did someone shoot him?"

"It was an accident," Eagle Hunter explained. "A man was sighting his bow and his hand slipped. The arrow hit the Hunt Chief."

Everybody turned to watch as the head medicine man came out of the house. He nodded to the crowd. The people knew the healing ceremony had been a success. The Hunt Chief would be all right. The medicine men had great powers.

As the hot, dry weather continued, the people of the village began to conserve as much water as possible. Soon it would be time for the late summer rains. But if they did not come, the water that had been saved would have to last a long time.

Each morning the women and girls made the long trip to the spring at the head of the canyon. The water, which had collected during the night in the natural shale basin, was carefully dipped into the water jars.

When the jars were full, the women placed donut-shaped, yucca-fiber pads on their heads. The heavy black and white jars were balanced on these pads, which left their hands free to climb the toe-and-hand notches of the cliff.

When the rains did not come, the priests announced the ceremonies which would be performed to ask the cloud god for rain. For several days, the chanting, accompanied by turtle-shell rattles, could be heard throughout the canyon. First the ceremonies took place in the secrecy of the kivas, but later the priests performed for the watching people in the court-yards.

One morning, shortly after the rain ceremonies, Little Fox and Gray Owl awoke to the rumble of distant thunder.

"Hurry, Gray Owl," Little Fox said, jumping up from his mat. "That thunder means the rain will be here soon. We must check the dams before it begins."

Quickly, they left the village, just as the wind started to blow with strong gusts down the canyon. The trees swayed frantically, as if an unseen hand were shaking them. The boys did not take long to complete their task because they did not want to be caught without shelter when the lightning and thunder came closer.

Back in the village, they watched as the wind

died down and everything became still. They could now see the large cloud hovering over the canyon. The earth grew dark, waiting.

"This will be a male rain. It will be hard," Little Fox explained to Gray Owl. "It is not like the female rains of spring, gentle and mild."

Suddenly the rain came pouring down. A wall of water shot over the front of the cave and crashed on the refuse heap below. Curtains of rain were blown down the canyon by the strong wind. Lightning zigzagged across the sky. The thunder crashed and boomed. It echoed off the canyon walls.

The people watched with awe from the shelter of the great cave. Occasionally, a gust of wind would carry a sprinkle of rain into their upturned faces.

Before long, the violent part of the storm moved down the canyon, and the rain gradually stopped.

"Come, Little Fox and Gray Owl," Eagle Hunter said, "we must check the fields to see what damage the rain has done."

The rain clouds had blown away, and the sun was shining on a dripping world by the time they reached the mesa. They were relieved to see that little damage had been done to the crops. It only took a short time to straighten the stalks of corn which had been blown down.

· Chapter VIII ·

The Green Corn Festival

Now that the rains of summer had started, the people of the cliff village would not have to worry about water. They knew they could expect showers every day or so. The weather had become cooler. A hint of fall was in the air.

Little Fox and Gray Owl continued to watch the fields. The ears of corn were big and fat. The bean pods were almost bursting with beans. The yellow squash dotted the fields.

"The green corn is ready," Eagle Hunter said one evening, as they were preparing to leave the field for the evening meal. "We will take some for White Flower to cook."

"The new corn is sweet and tender," Little Fox told Gray Owl. "There are many ways to cook it."

He helped his father check the fattest ears and pull off those which had dried silk hanging from the tops.

"What color is the corn now?" asked Gray Owl, as he followed Little Fox down the rows.

The cornstalks towered above their heads.

"It is all white," Little Fox answered. "It will not be different colors until it has become dry."

That evening White Flower baked the ears of corn in the fire. The pot of deer stew was almost forgotten. They were tired of it, but the corn was delicious.

"Pull the husks off this way," explained Little Fox. He helped Gray Owl peel the dry, burned outer layers of husks away from the juicy kernels inside.

When the meal was finished, sighs of contentment from all the family members agreed there was nothing like the first corn of the fall!

Every day after that, the boys brought the ears of corn to the village as they ripened. They also helped pick the beans and squash. With a sling hung over their backs, they were able to carry several ears of corn or several fat squash at a time down the cliff.

White Flower, Blue Bird and Butterfly Girl were busy roasting the corn and grinding it into a fine meal to be mixed with water later in the winter. This hot drink would be welcome when the snows came. All over the village, women were using the small stones to grind the corn against the larger stones.

One day while Little Fox and Gray Owl were picking corn, the men of the village began to dig

large pits close to the cornfields.

"What are they doing?" asked Gray Owl.

"Tomorrow is the day that has been set by the Village Chief for the Green Corn Festival," Little Fox replied. "Come, we will help the men gather firewood."

The boys helped drag limbs and sticks to the pit near their field. They helped pick hundreds of ears of corn and piled it nearby. A fire was kept burning all night in the pit.

The next morning everyone in the village who could climb the cliff went to the mesa top. The men scraped the ashes out of the hot pits which were then lined with cornstalks and leaves. Afterwards, everyone helped toss in the corn, then covered it with more cornstalks and finally sealed it with soil.

While the corn was steaming in these large "ovens," the women and girls built small fires to prepare other types of food.

Little Fox and Gray Owl gathered with the other boys and young men. They watched a wrestling contest between two of the older boys. After that, they tried their skill in shooting a bow and arrow at a target. But the foot race was what they were waiting for.

"I know you can win," Little Fox said, as Gray Owl got into position at the starting mark.

Running Deer was also there. He would never miss a foot race.

"Gray Owl, you can not keep up with me this time," he bragged. "I will run away from you."

"Just wait and see," Little Fox said. He did not think anyone could run as fast as his friend, Gray Owl.

The starter gave a shout and the racers were off. Their bare feet stirred up a cloud of dust as they sprinted toward the large juniper tree which marked halfway. A crowd of people had gathered to watch.

"Come on, Gray Owl, you can do it," Little Fox called, as the racers rounded the tree and started back toward the group of spectators.

Little Fox could see that Running Deer was in front. Gray Owl was close behind, straining forward. Just before they dashed across the finish line, he pulled ahead of Running Deer, whose light, brown face was a shade darker with embarrassment and disappointment. He had always been the winner of the race during the Green Corn Festival. "You never would have won, if I had not hurt my foot," Running Deer said, scowling at Gray Owl. He dashed away.

Just then Eagle Hunter called to them, "The corn is ready." The thought of food drove the race and its outcome out of their minds as the pit near their field was opened and the steaming corn was passed out.

After all had eaten their fill, they settled back to watch the large, round moon rise over the mesa. They did not see it often because the cave hid it from view.

Later, by the brilliant light of the moon, the people wandered slowly back to the village.

Several days after the Green Corn Festival, Little Fox and Gray Owl came down from the mesa for the evening meal. But instead of finding White Flower at the fire, they found Blue Bird stirring the steaming pots.

"What has happened? Where is Mother?" asked Little Fox before he became aware of the activity around the door of their house. The women of the clan were coming and going quickly, chattering in excited voices.

Blue Bird smiled at the boys. "Mother has just had a baby boy," she said with pride. "She is well and the baby is healthy."

Little Fox gave a sigh of relief. He was glad to hear about his new brother. He knew care had been taken to do everything according to their beliefs. Before the baby was born, one of his mother's brothers had been chosen to go down into the kiva and release a spirit from the underworld. He would have removed the plug in the sipapu only long enough to allow one spirit to escape. That spirit would have entered the new baby boy.

"May we see my new brother?" Little Fox asked. "Yes," Blue Bird replied. She watched as the two boys went quietly through the low doorway.

White Flower was lying on a bed of animal skins. She gave them a tired but proud smile. Beside her lay the baby in a bed of warm sand. Juniper ashes had been smeared on his forehead to protect him from witches. Someone had placed a perfect ear of corn beside him.

"He is very little," Little Fox. He smiled as the baby waved his arms jerkily. "We can call him 'Little Baby.'"

White Flower understood the gentle teasing and smiled at each of her sons, in turn. "Well, we cannot name him yet, but though he is small, he will grow and then we will name him to help him grow up big and strong."

As the boys sat around the fire that night, Little Fox told Gray Owl more about the ritual for the new baby which would follow in the next few days.

"My mother and the baby will stay in the house for twenty days. They must have quiet and no bright light to hurt the baby's eyes. Then, every fifth day, the women of the clan will wash my mother's hair with yucca suds and bathe her with water. Juniper twigs will be boiled in the water before it is used to wash her."

Gray Owl asked, "What will happen then?"

"At sunrise on the twentieth day, the baby's head will be washed. He will be taken to the top of the cliff and dedicated to the Sun Father. That is the day he will receive his real name, not 'Little Baby' as we call him now. He will get a name from each aunt and his grandmother. Only one name will be used, though. After that, the baby will be placed on a wooden cradle board. He will stay there until it is time for him to walk."

Gray Owl sat still for a few minutes. He seemed to be thinking over what Little Fox had said.

"The baby was born with a round head," he said thoughtfully. "The hard cradle board must make the back of the head flat because the baby lies there for so long. Until he walks—that's a very long time."

"Do your people use a cradle board?" asked Little Fox.

"Yes," Gray Owl replied with a far-away look in his eyes. "But we place soft skins beneath the baby's head, so that it does not become flat."

Little Fox looked at his friend. Once again, he wanted to know what Gray Owl was thinking about as he gazed into the distance. Did he miss his people? Little Fox knew that he himself would be very sad if he were never to see his own home again.

· Chapter IX ·
The Harvest

"Hand me another basket of corn," Little Fox called to Gray Owl. "There is just room for one more."

Reluctantly, Gray Owl climbed to where Little Fox was standing. There was barely room for the two boys on the edge of a rock shelf in the tiny storage cave. Each time he had climbed there with a basket of corn, Gray Owl had looked frightened. The height did not bother Little Fox. He was used to storing corn in the high shelves of the cliff.

Both boys had been working for days helping to fill every available crevice in the rocks. This year the harvest had been good. But if next year were bad, they would need this carefully stored food.

Little Fox finished sealing the small cave with rocks, and the boys started down the cliff.

Suddenly, Gray Owl's foot slipped. A shower of small stones rolled down the rock face.

"I am going to fall," cried Gray Owl, hanging by his fingers. He turned his panic-stricken face toward Little Fox. "What can I do?"

"Place your feet in that crack beside you,"

Little Fox said, pointing to a small fissure in the rock.

Slowly, Gray Owl inched sideways until he could reach the crack. Carefully, placing one foot after the other, he made his way to the bottom of the cliff.

"From now on, I will carry the squash down to the village," he said with a shaky laugh. "At least I am used to *that* cliff," he laughed again, but he was obviously proud of his accomplishment.

"Mother should have some beans ready for storage," said Little Fox. "Come, we can help her with that."

When the boys reached the mesa, they saw White Flower beating the ground with a large stick. Blue Bird and Butterfly Girl were doing the same nearby.

"What are they doing?" asked Gray Owl.

"They are beating the dry pods off the beans," Little Fox explained.

The mass of beans and broken pods on the hard ground was put into a yucca-fiber basket by White Flower. When it was full, she held it high above her head then slowly leaned forward and emptied the basket on the ground. The breeze blowing over the mesa carried the lighter pods away and the beans fell at her feet.

The boys filled a basket with the clean beans

and started back toward the canyon rim.
Butterfly Girl followed with yet another basket.

A few minutes later when they reached the
village, they stopped to watch the busy people.
The evidence of a good harvest could be seen
everywhere. The rooftops and courtyards were
a riot of color. The brilliantly tinted ears of corn
had been piled in every available space. They
had been dried and their many colors could be
seen: red, black, blue, yellow, white, and
speckled. Large ears of corn were hanging from
the roof poles. Piles of green and yellow squash
made pools of color against the buff stone of the
houses. Heaps of dark brown beans added their

accent to the golden harvest colors.

Everywhere the women and girls were busy getting the harvest ready for storage. Some were cutting the squash into strips to be dried. Others were husking the large ears of corn, or turning the corn so it would dry properly.

In addition to the crops, the women and girls had been busy gathering wild foods to add variety to their meals. Bundles of drying herbs were hanging on the walls of the houses. Near each house sat jars full of roots, fruits, seeds and berries collected from the nearby mesa and canyons. Baskets of pinyon nuts were being stored with care. These nuts were a favorite food for the winter months.

"We will have plenty of food for winter," Little Fox told Gray Owl. They walked through the busy village carrying their basket of beans. "Soon it will be time for the fall hunts to begin. Already there has been some talk that large herds of deer and mountain sheep have been moving back into the area."

"Will we be able to go on a hunt?" asked Gray Owl.

"We will ask Father," Little Fox replied.

That evening when Eagle Hunter had finished eating, Little Fox asked him about the hunt.

"The Hunt Chief is planning a large hunt for

tomorrow," Eagle Hunter said. "You may go."

Far into the night, the boys listened to the chanting coming from the kivas. The men and older boys were performing the ceremonies that would insure a successful hunt.

The next morning, the excited boys were up at sunrise. They joined the men and other boys as they prepared their weapons.

"Gray Owl, I have something for you," Little Fox's uncle said, handing Gray Owl a small stone the shape of a mountain lion.

"All the hunters carry the image of an animal which is a good hunter," Little Fox said. "See, I have an eagle. These carvings will bring us good luck."

As soon as everyone was ready, the hunters trotted off to a distant canyon where large herds of animals had been seen browsing. The hunting party split into two smaller groups. They moved quietly up two canyons which were parallel to each other. The Hunt Chief gave a shout and the men and boys ran up the sides of the canyons and formed a large circle on the flat mesa. They began to shout and thrash in the bushes. The circle of hunters became smaller and smaller, squeezing the frightened animals into a small area. When an animal tried to escape from the circle, it was killed. Each time an animal was killed, a prayer was said to its spirit. The hunters knew the animal would understand that it was helping the people of the mesa to live.

When an animal was killed, a downy feather was placed on its body to make it lighter, as the hard task of carrying the meat back to the village began.

When the meat had been carried to the village, the women and girls began the process of preparing it for storage. They cut long strips to be dried over slow fires. The skin would be made into fine leather and the bones into tools. Every bit of the animal would be used.

Little Fox and Gray Owl were helping Eagle Hunter carry his deer when Running Deer came close. "Where is your deer?" he asked. "I killed one and it is ready to carry back to the village."

"I did not have a chance to get mine," Little Fox said.

"I am a good hunter," Running Deer bragged, as he stalked off. "Not everyone is."

"Do not worry, Little Fox. You will make your kill next time," Gray Owl said. "There will be other hunts."

After the hunt, the weather turned colder. Some mornings there was a thin sheet of snow on the ground. By midday, it would be gone, but it was a sign of things to come.

One cold morning, Eagle Hunter set out the materials needed to make feather blankets. Some were made from cotton, which had been brought by the trader from the south, but the turkey feather blankets were warmer.

"How do you keep the feathers together?" asked Gray Owl when he saw the large pile of small, fluffy, brown feathers.

Little Fox pointed to some heavy yucca cord. "This will be used," he said. "But we will help Father. That is the best way to see how the blankets are made."

"First, the feathers are split down the middle,"

explained Eagle Hunter. "Then they are wrapped very tightly around the cord."

Gray Owl watched as a long, feather rope took shape.

"When we have enough rope, we will weave it into a blanket," Eagle Hunter said.

It was a slow task, but the two boys stuck to it until they had enough rope for a blanket.

"This blanket will be for Gray Owl," Eagle Hunter said. "He does not have one."

When the feather blankets were done, Eagle Hunter turned to the job of making cotton blankets to be worn under the feather ones. Sometimes the ends of the feathers worked loose. They were scratchy. A cotton blanket next to the skin would feel good.

White Flower, Blue Bird and Butterfly Girl had also been busy during this time. They had used bone awls and needles to sew the soft, tanned deer, mountain sheep and rabbit skins into slip-over jackets and robes. Short leggings were also made from leather to keep the legs warm during the winter.

After several days, Eagle Hunter decided there were enough blankets and clothes for the family. Little Fox and Gray Owl sat back to rest their fingers. They were proudly surveying their work, when they noticed White Flower hurrying toward them.

Grandfather is sick," she cried. "We must get the medicine man."

While Eagle Hunter went to get help, Little Fox ran to the old man, who was lying near the fire.

"Grandfather," he whispered softly, "the medicine man will be here soon. He will make you well." There was no response from the old man.

· Chapter X ·
Grandfather

~~~~~~~~~~~~~~~~~~~~~~~~~~~~~~~~~~~

With the help of Little Fox's uncle, Eagle Hunter carried Grandfather down into his family kiva. The boys could hear the chants of the medicine man as he worked with the old man.

"He will be all right, won't he?" asked Little Fox when he saw the worried look on White Flower's face.

"I do not know," she replied. "He is very old."

Much later, the medicine man came up the ladder from the kiva. "Right now he is breathing easier," he said to White Flower. "But he must stay down there where it is warm."

The next morning when Little Fox and Gray Owl crawled out of their warm blankets, the ground outside the cave was covered with snow. The trees in the canyon below were bent over with the weight of the soft, white mantle.

"We finished the blankets just in time," Little Fox said when they gathered around the fire for the morning meal. "How is Grandfather?" he asked his mother.

They could hear the soft chanting coming from the kiva.

"He is still very ill," White Flower said. She was grinding corn on a large, grooved stone. "The medicine men have prayed over him all night."

Little Fox and Gray Owl sat and listened to the chanting. The bow they intended to repair lay forgotten at their feet. The medicine men came and went throughout the day.

Just as the evening shadows began to fall on the snow outside the cave, White Flower came over to where Little Fox was sitting.

"The medicine men have not been able to help your grandfather. He is dead," she said softly. Tears glistened in her brown eyes.

"I am sorry," Gray Owl said, placing his hand on Little Fox's arm.

"We will prepare his body for burial tomorrow," White Flower said, as she returned to the fire.

That evening, the rest of the family sat silent and sad, huddled close to the fire for warmth, while White Flower talked about her father. She told them how he would always bring home a deer during the hunt and how fine the corn was in his fields. Little Fox had an empty feeling inside while she talked. His grandfather was gone.

When the clan gathered around the fire the next morning, the day was gray and snow was still falling silently outside. White Flower and her brothers decided that, since his spirit would leave the body, their father would be buried in the refuse heap in the back of the cave. There, he would still be a part of the family. His arms and legs were folded close to his body. He was wrapped in a cotton blanket and then in a larger feather blanket. The final covering was a piece of matting.

After the grave was dug in the soft material of the refuse heap, his body was placed in it. Food and water were also placed in the shallow grave. All of Grandfather's favorite weapons, tools and jewelry were put beside his body. The grave was covered.

For four days the family placed food and water on the grave. The spirit would not leave the body until the four days had passed. After the fourth day, the spirit would return to the Mother Earth through the sipapu.

There were always deaths in the village, especially in the winter. The people knew they were to be accepted.

Shortly after Grandfather's death, the snow began to melt.

"We will need more firewood before the next snow comes," White FLower said to Little Fox. "Today would be a good day to get some from the mesa."

"Come, Gray Owl, we will get the firewood," Little Fox said.

"Will you take Running Deer with you?" White Flower asked. "He has been very sad since Grandfather's death."

The three boys and Dog set off across the mesa. They had to walk for quite a distance to find firewood. The people of the village had been gathering it near the cave. The ground under their feet was soft and mushy due to the melted snow. The sun was warm. It was a relief to be out of the cold, damp cave for a short time.

A rabbit bounded out of a brush pile in front of them. Before they could get their arrows into their bows, it had disappeared.

"It would have been good to have some rabbit stew for the evening meal," Little Fox said. "We must watch for another one."

"I will be ready next time," Running Deer said.

Just then, they heard a rustling noise in the brush ahead.

"There is one now," Running Deer said, advancing toward the noise.

"Be careful," Little Fox whispered. "You cannot see what is in there."

Slowly the three boys crept forward. Running Deer was in the lead. He stopped and raised his bow. But it was not a rabbit the startled boys saw. It was a large yellow cat.

It was crouching on the limb of a juniper tree just above Running Deer's head.

"It is a mountain lion," Little Fox cried. "Run."

But Running Deer stood as if turned to stone. A rumble came from the throat of the cat. It crept farther out on the limb, its muscles tensing for the leap which would bring it down on top of Running Deer.

Suddenly an arrow whizzed by Little Fox. It hit the limb under the mountain lion with a thud. The startled animal drew back. It leaped to one side of the boys and ran with great, long strides through the trees.

"That was close," Little Fox said with relief. "He could have killed you, Running Deer. It was a good thing Gray Owl had his bow ready."

"If he had not shot, I would have killed the mountain lion with my bow and arrow," Running Deer said angrily.

"Oh, Running Deer, when will you ever learn? Gray Owl wants to be your friend. He was trying to help you."

"I do not need his help," Running Deer replied. He frowned and angrily strode off through the woods.

Little Fox and Gray Owl followed, stopping to gather sticks of firewood on their way back to the village.

The next day, the cold winds blew down the canyon bringing another snow storm. Icicles froze on the overhang of the cave. The people stayed close to the fires in the courtyard.

The long, winter days were spent sleeping late and staying close to the fires. The men and older boys spent the biggest part of their time in the kivas, performing ceremonies and gambling. The children invented games to pass the time. Sometimes these games included teasing the turkeys and chasing the dogs. Every mother in the village was looking forward to spring, when the children could once more play in the canyon or on the mesa.

Little Fox and Gray Owl spent a great part of each day listening to Little Fox's uncle. He told them about their people when they first settled on the mesa. They had lived in the caves first and then had moved to the mesa tops. There they built houses and grew their crops. It was only in recent years that they had moved back into the caves to build their stone cities.

As the winter months wore on, sickness and more deaths occurred. Winter was especially hard on the older people. Their joints became swollen and painful from the cold and dampness.

Toward the end of winter, the snow disappeared and the air became warmer. The people began to stir and think of the activities which come with the spring. The buds on the trees and bushes were beginning to swell and tiny, green sprouts of grass were appearing. Animals, that had not been seen all winter, were coming out of their dens. The long, cold, winter months were ending.

As the weather became warmer, Little Fox, Gray Owl and Running Deer went more often to the mesa. Soon it would be time to prepare the fields for the spring planting. But the soil had not yet dried out enough for that, so the boys were able to roam the canyons and mesas.

One morning, just as Little Fox and Gray Owl were finishing the morning meal, Running Deer hurried over to them.

"I have heard of an owl's nest in a cave not far from here," he said. "Will you help me find it?"

"Yes, we will help you," Little Fox replied. He bent to push a burning stick into the fire. The flame leaped up close to his hand. He jerked it back.

"Did you burn your hand?" Gray Owl asked. He looked at the angry, red spot on the palm of Little Fox's hand.

"It will be all right shortly," Little Fox said. "Come, we will try to find the owl's nest."

A short time later, the three boys stood looking down a sheer rock face to the canyon floor far below.

"The cave where the owl has a nest is about halfway down the cliff," Running Deer explained. He was pointing straight down.

"We can not climb down there. It is too steep, and there are no notches for our hands and toes," Little Fox said.

"I did not think you were afraid to climb any cliff anywhere, Little Fox," Running Deer said. "You are afraid just like Gray Owl." He turned his back to the cliff and eased his body over the edge. His feet dangled in space. "I will go by myself. I am not afraid."

Little Fox and Gray Owl lay down on their stomachs and peered over the edge of the cliff as Running Deer slowly inched his way down the rock. He was just a short distance from them when his foot slipped.

The two boys at the top had only a glimpse of the look of terror on Running Deer's face, as he half-slid and half-fell down the cliff.

· Chapter XI ·
The Old Trader Returns

Little Fox and Gray Owl could only watch helplessly as Running Deer fell.

"Look, he has landed on a ledge," Gray Owl cried. "The rock that broke loose is falling toward him."

"Running Deer, are you all right?" called Little Fox. He listened anxiously for an answer, but none came.

"What are we going to do?" Gray Owl asked. "We must help him."

"Help, help." A weak cry came from the ledge. Little Fox breathed a sigh of relief. At least Running Deer was still alive. But how badly was he hurt?

"I must climb down and help him," Little Fox said. He hung his feet over the edge of the cliff. "Oh, the burn on my hand hurts. I cannot do it."

"I will have to help him," Gray Owl whispered.

"But you are not used to climbing such a

sheer cliff," Little Fox cried. "You will fall too."

"There is no one else," Gray Owl said. With a determined look on his face, he lay down on his stomach and swung his legs over the edge. Carefully he eased his feet down until he could reach a small notch below.

"Move to the left a little," coached Little Fox. "There is a small shelf."

With his feet on the shelf and his fingers using tiny depressions in the stone, Gray Owl moved slowly to the left until he reached a notch where he could put his toes. Making one slow move at a time, he crept down the rock face.

It seemed like a long time before Little Fox

heard Gray Owl shout, "I have reached him. A large rock has fallen on his leg. I will move it."

Little Fox felt helpless as he waited at the top of the cliff. Of all days to hurt his hand, this was the worst.

"Running Deer has hurt his leg," called Gray Owl. "We will need to get him out of here."

"I will go to the village," Little Fox called.

Never had his short legs moved so fast, as he ran through the trees. When he reached the mesa, he found Running Deer's father and some other men of their clan.

"Hurry," he called breathlessly. "Running Deer has fallen down a cliff. We need a rope to reach him."

It did not take the men long to bring a rope made of the strong fibers of the yucca plant. Carrying it, they hurried across the mesa.

"Gray Owl is down there on the ledge with Running Deer," Little Fox explained when they reached the cliff. "He climbed down when I could not."

"He has been very brave," said Running Deer's father. "It could not have been easy for him."

In a short time, the rope was lowered to the ledge. Running Deer's father climbed down. Before long, Gray Owl's head appeared at the edge of the cliff.

Little Fox helped him to the mesa top. He could feel Gray Owl shaking. No, it had not been easy for Gray Owl to climb down there, but he had done it to help Running Deer.

Quickly, Running Deer's father climbed up the rope with the scraped and bruised boy on his back. The rock had left a raw, bleeding place on his leg. Other than that, he seemed to be all right.

Running Deer looked at Gray Owl. "Thank you for helping me," he said. "I am sorry for the way I have treated you. I would like to be your friend. Father, could we ask the Council to make Gray Owl a member of the tribe?"

"Yes," his father answered. "We would welcome Gray Owl into our tribe and our clan."

Later that evening, a group of children gathered close to the fire. Running Deer was the center of attention. He lay on a mat, his scrapes and bruises covered with the healing herbs used by the medicine men. The story of the accident was told over and over again. Each time it was told, the children looked with admiring eyes at Gray Owl. Little Fox was proud of his friend. He was a very brave boy. Now he would become one of them just as Little Fox had hoped.

But the next morning, before the Council could meet to make their decision, the old trader came back.

When he saw Gray Owl, he stared in amazement. "Little Antelope, I did not think I would ever see you again. Your people told me you had disappeared. They feared you were dead."

"You have seen my people?" Gray Owl asked eagerly. "Where are they now?"

"They have made camp on the flat land near the mountains," the old man explained.

Little Fox looked at the face of his friend. There was a look of joy shining on it. How he must have missed his people and his own way of life. What was it the trader called him? Little Antelope. That must have been the name he used when they first met, but Little Fox could not understand his language.

The trader and Gray Owl were still talking. Little Fox began to listen to them.

"Your grandfather is getting very old," the trader was saying. "Who will be the chief of your tribe when he dies?"

"My uncle will be chief," Gray Owl said.

"Your uncle was killed on a hunt not long ago," the trader replied. "Now there is no one."

"I did not like my uncle, but I am sorry to hear he is dead," said Gray Owl sadly.

Gray Owl turned to Little Fox to explain. "My father would have been chief, but when he was killed, my uncle did not think I would be able to lead our people. He was ready to take over when Grandfather was gone. That is one of the reasons I left."

"What will you do?" asked Little Fox. "You can become one of my people. You are my friend, and I am yours. I do not want you to leave."

"My people need me to teach them what I have learned here," Gray Owl said. "I have learned how you plant crops, make pottery and many other things. All of these are important. But the most important thing I have learned is that a person who is different from another can become a real friend. You have taught me that, Little Fox."

"I believe our whole village has found that out, too," Little Fox said, looking at Running Deer and the other children. "A person may look different on the outside, but we are all the same on the inside. I will miss you, Gray Owl—" He stopped and laughed. "I cannot stop calling you that! I named you Gray Owl because you looked like a little fox, the way I wanted to look. I looked like a little owl, so I gave you my name. It will be hard for me to call you 'Little Antelope' when you will always be my friend 'Gray Owl.'" He shook his head in resignation. "I will miss you, my friend, but I understand why you must return to your own people. When will you leave?"

Gray Owl looked eagerly toward the trader.

"I will be traveling back toward the mountains before the sun is high tomorrow," the old man said with a smile.

That night a crowd gathered around the fire for the evening meal. White Flower was busy putting out food enough for everyone. The baby was propped in his cradle board nearby, his bright button eyes watching all that was happening. Blue Bird and Butterfly Girl were helping with the cooking pots, while Eagle Hunter sat bartering with the trader for a pouch of salt. Running Deer and his parents were there as well. Word had spread that Gray Owl was leaving and many came with gifts for him: a seashell necklace, a turkey feather blanket, a new bow, a pot with black and white design.

The next morning, just as the light began to filter into the cave, Little Fox watched his friend and the trader start down the sheer face of the cliff. Gray Owl tilted up his face, waved to Little Fox and called to him. Little Fox turned back to the village as Running Deer limped toward him.

"Come, let us eat so we will be ready to help clear the fields for the spring planting," Little Fox said, putting his hand on Running Deer's shoulder.

Running Deer turned toward him. "I heard Gray Owl call to you, but I could not hear his words. What did he say?"

"He said," Little Fox smiled gently, his eyes glistening, "that one day Little Antelope would return, and when he did, we would know that Gray Owl had come home again." The boys turned into the rising sun, reveling in the new day.

· Bibliography ·

BALDWIN, Gordon C. *The Ancient Ones*. New York: W. W. Norton & Company, Inc., 1963.

LANCASTER, James A., *et al*. *Archeological Excavations in Mesa Verde National Park, Colorado*. Archeological Research Series No. 2, National Park Service. Washington, D. C.: United States Department of the Interior, 1954.

Reader's Digest. "America's Fascinating Indian Heritage." Pleasantville, N.Y.: The Reader's Digest Association, Inc., 1978.

SOLOMON, Julian Harris. *The Book of Indian Crafts & Indian Lore*. New York: Harper & Brothers, 1928.

SIMPSON, Ruth DeEtte. *The Hopi Indian*. Los Angeles, Calif.: Southwest Museum, Leaflet No. 25, 1971.

WATSON, Don. *Indians of the Mesa Verde*. Mesa Verde National Park, Colorado: Mesa Verde Museum Association, 1961.

WORMINGTON, H. M. *Prehistoric Indians of the Southwest*. Denver, Colorado: The Denver Museum of Natural History, Series No. 7, 1961.

· The Author ·
Ida May Hobbs

Born and raised near Tunelton, West Virginia, Ida May Hobbs earned a Bachelor of Arts degree in Education at Fairmont State College.

Two summer seasons at Mesa Verde National Park working for the Chief Ranger caught Mrs. Hobbs in the web of enchantment that Mesa Verde spins. The many hours she spent in the cliff dwellings sparked her imagination as she wondered what it might have been like to live at Mesa Verde during the time the cliff dwellers flourished. That wondering was the beginning of this book, *The Coming of Gray Owl*.

Presently living with two of her four daughters in Gatlinburg, Tennessee, Mrs. Hobbs works as a seasonal park ranger at the Great Smoky Mountains National Park.